EXTREME JOBS IN EXTREME PLACES

LIFE AT A
POLAR RESEARCH STATION

By Arthur K. Britton

Gareth Stevens
Publishing

D0201930

Please visit our website, www.garethstevens.com. For a free color catalog of all our high-quality books, call toll free 1-800-542-2595 or fax 1-877-542-2596.

Library of Congress Cataloging-in-Publication Data

Britton, Arthur K.
 Life at a polar research station / Arthur K. Britton.
     p. cm. — (Extreme jobs in extreme places)
 Includes index.
 ISBN 978-1-4339-8483-9 (pbk.)
 ISBN 978-1-4339-8484-6 (6-pack)
 ISBN 978-1-4339-8482-2 (library binding)
 1. Biological stations—Antarctica—Juvenile literature. 2. Research teams—Antarctica—Juvenile literature. 3. Polar regions—Research—Juvenile literature. I. Title.
 QH323.A6B75 2013
 570.72—dc23
                                        2012021199

First Edition

Published in 2013 by
Gareth Stevens Publishing
111 East 14th Street, Suite 349
New York, NY 10003

Copyright © 2013 Gareth Stevens Publishing

Designer: Andrea Davison-Bartolotta
Editor: Therese M. Shea

Photo credits: Cover, p. 1 Thomas J. Abercrombie/National Geographic/Getty Images; p. 4 AridOcean/Shutterstock.com; pp. 5, 7 Armin Rose/Shutterstock.com; p. 6 courtesy of Jens Dreyer/National Science Foundation; p. 8 courtesy of Corey Anthony/National Science Foundation; p. 9 courtesy of Joe Harrigan/National Science Foundation; pp. 11, 14, 17, 18, 21 courtesy of Peter Rejcek/National Science Foundation; p. 12 courtesy of Dr. Stacy Kim/National Science Foundation; p. 13 Gordon Wiltsie/National Geographic/Getty Images; p. 15 courtesy of John Mallon III/National Science Foundation; p. 16 courtesy of Mark Sabbatini/National Science Foundation; p. 19 courtesy of Ginny Figlar/National Science Foundation; p. 20 courtesy of Emily Stone/National Science Foundation; p. 21 (inset) courtesy of Robyn Waserman/National Science Foundation; p. 23 courtesy of Dr. Will Silva/National Science Foundation; p. 24 courtesy of Bill Meurer/National Science Foundation; p. 25 courtesy of Lane Patterson/National Science Foundation; p. 27 courtesy of John Goodge/National Science Foundation; p. 28 courtesy of Stephen Kish/National Science Foundation; p. 29 courtesy of Patrick Cullis/National Science Foundation.

Printed in the United States of America

CPSIA compliance information: Batch #CS13GS: For further information contact Gareth Stevens, New York, New York at 1-800-542-2595.

CONTENTS

Words in the glossary appear in **bold** type the first time they are used in the text.

THE BOTTOM OF THE WORLD

Antarctica is one of the most extreme places on Earth. It surrounds the South Pole at the bottom of the world. Thick layers of ice and snow cover Antarctica. It's extremely cold. Winter temperatures reach –94°F (–70°C). In summer, it rarely gets above freezing. Winds that can exceed 100 miles (160 km) per hour make it feel much colder.

Dark and light are extreme in Antarctica, too. For several months in winter, it's always dark. In summer, the sun never sets!

Would you like to live there? Probably not. But some people go enthusiastically. They work at polar **research** stations.

Africa

South America

Antarctica

Australia

HIDDEN ANTARCTICA

Antarctica's ice and snow are more than 2 miles (3.2 km) thick in places. The land can look like an empty plain. But appearances can fool you. Underneath the ice and snow, there are mountains and deep valleys. Antarctica even has volcanoes! In some places, deep cracks called crevasses split the ice.

ANTARCTIC RESEARCH STATIONS

Today, Antarctica is home to more than 40 research stations operated by 18 countries from around the world. Some stations are small, while others are large. For example, England's Halley Research Station currently has seven buildings. The United States' McMurdo Station has about 85 buildings.

Many stations are built near the coast or on nearby islands. This makes it easier for people and supplies to reach them. In some places, the station buildings are on poles that raise them above the snow and ice. This is to keep them from being buried by snow or even crushed by the snow's weight.

▲ Amundsen-Scott South Pole Station

Some research stations use wind energy to produce the electricity they need.

EXTREME BUILDINGS

Heavy snow crushed early buildings at England's Halley Research Station. So engineers created extreme buildings. Three rested on platforms with steel legs. They were raised annually to keep them above the snow. Two rested on skis and were towed to a new position yearly. When work began on new buildings in 2008, these practices continued.

The station buildings have laboratories for scientists. They have places to keep snowmobiles and other **equipment**. Of course, the stations also have places for people to sleep and eat.

What happens at these stations? Research, naturally! Scientists go to Antarctica to do all kinds of research. They study the ocean, weather, **climate change**, biology, **geology**, and even astronomy. And scientists aren't the only people at the stations. People with many different skills are needed to keep the stations running smoothly and make the research possible. Let's take a look at what some of the jobs are like at an Antarctic research station.

MCMURDO STATION

McMurdo Station is the largest Antarctic research station. About 1,000 people live there in summer, while only about 250 people spend the winter there. MacTown, as people call it, is built on bare rock on Ross Island. The buildings include restaurants and a radio station. It also has a harbor, airport, and landing pad for helicopters.

MCMURDO STATION
ANTARCTICA

McMurdo Station, shown here, sits along the coastline of Ross Island, which was formed by volcanoes.

EXTREMELY COLD SCIENCE

When you're a scientist in Antarctica, even getting dressed is extreme. Several layers of lightweight clothing are needed to provide the required warmth and freedom of movement. Imagine how long it takes to get dressed!

Even scientists' equipment may need "clothing" for protection from the extreme cold. For example, mitten-like cases may be used to keep cameras from freezing.

Simple tasks become hard when you're working in extremely cold, windy conditions. Fingers become painful, stop working, and freeze. Work at higher elevations adds another challenge. The air has less oxygen, so every motion requires more effort.

DOUBLE DUTY

Since most Antarctic research stations have only a small number of people, everyone—even the scientists—must be able and willing to perform more than one job. For example, a **meteorologist** who flies to a distant weather station might need to help fly the plane and even help refuel it.

This scientist takes notes at a camp near McMurdo Station. A team has been conducting a study of a seal population there.

Scientists sometimes work in the field. That is, they work at a location far from the research station. They may go for a few days or as long as 3 months. So where do scientists live while they're working in the field? In tents!

Of course, their tents aren't like ordinary camping tents. They're specially made to stand up to the high winds and sharp grains of ice blown by the winds. An airbed, sheepskin, and special ground sheet provide protection from the cold ground. Scientists sleep in extra thick and warm sleeping bags, too.

research field camp

LYING UP

Sometimes scientists in the field encounter extremely high winds or whiteouts, where fog—perhaps with rain or snow—makes it impossible to see. At such times, they're unable to work, and it's dangerous to even leave the tents. So scientists stay inside doing whatever work they can. This is called "lying up."

13

KEEPING STATIONS WORKING

The scientists' research is only possible because of the work done by the support staff. There are usually four or five **technical** staff members for every scientist.

One important technical person is the machinist. A machinist is someone who uses machine tools to make parts. In Antarctica, a machinist makes parts for research equipment. Not only is such equipment specialized, but, of course, it also has to work in extreme conditions. For example, there are telescopes that must be able to endure temperatures as low as –100°F (–73°C)!

What happens when scientists' electronic instruments break down? Fortunately, there are electronics technicians to repair them.

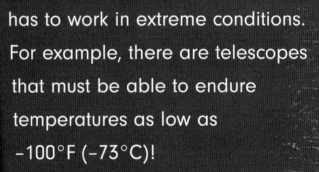
technician works on heating system

This construction crew stands in front of the South Pole Telescope, which they assembled. The telescope will help in studies of deep space.

GETTING A STATION STARTED

Before research can begin, the station must be built. That takes several years. Beginning in 2007, crews at Belgium's Princess Elisabeth Antarctic Station lived in tents while constructing the garages and main building. The next year, they built furniture and set up equipment. The station officially opened in 2009.

15

Each station must provide for itself the basic goods and services usually supplied by businesses and governments. For example, you buy electricity from a power company. In Antarctica, there are no power companies. Each station must produce its own electricity. It uses **generators**, batteries, solar power, wind power, or a combination of these.

Making sure the electrical system operates properly is extremely important. Not only does the research depend on it, so do people's lives. The person with this huge responsibility is the station engineer. The engineer oversees all other technical systems, too. Engineers also set up and operate instruments for scientists' research.

FIRST ON THE SCENE

Belgium's Princess Elisabeth Antarctic Station doesn't operate during the winter. When spring arrives, a small team goes to the station. They start the bulldozers and remove snow. They turn on a generator, test systems, and get the communication equipment operating. Once the station is up and running, everyone else begins to arrive.

transporting equipment by sled ▶

An engineer checks on the many systems that keep McMurdo Station running smoothly.

Water is necessary for life. Humans can't survive long without drinking water. People also use water for cooking. Modern conveniences such as showers and toilets require water. However, getting water in Antarctica isn't easy. In fact, there's an engineer in charge of water at research stations.

On the frozen continent, there's very little liquid freshwater. A water production system melts snow to make water for drinking, cooking, bathing, and toilets. Wastewater must be dealt with, too. Just dumping it outside would harm Antarctica's **ecosystem**. To handle this matter, stations have water treatment systems.

EXTREME PHOTOGRAPHER

In this book, you've seen pictures of Antarctic research stations. You can find many more online. Have you wondered who takes them? Scientists and staff members take some. However, sometimes there's a photographer whose job is to record life and research at the station. Just imagine how hard that is in this extremely cold, windy land!

This technician takes samples from the McMurdo water plant to test the water's purity.

FRESH WATER
TANK 1

Antarctic research stations have bulldozers for clearing snow and other **vehicles** for hauling people and equipment. Even under the best conditions, vehicles need regular maintenance and repair. Vehicles in Antarctica's extreme conditions need even more care. So research stations have **mechanics**. When they're not caring for vehicles, the mechanics work on the station's technical systems.

Mechanics and other staff also help with less interesting, though important, tasks. They repair tents, clean the station surroundings after work, sort waste, and prepare waste vessels to be taken to the coast and shipped out. There's always work to be done.

GAs AND GFAs

Interested in experiencing life and work in Antarctica? Even without special skills, you can. Stations have workers called general assistants (GAs) or general field assistants (GFAs). GAs help with ordinary tasks. They shovel snow, clean up, and do anything else they're asked to. The work may not sound exciting, but it's a great way to see Antarctica!

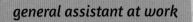

general assistant at work

This vehicle hauls two tanks filled with substances used to fight fires at an Antarctic research station.

CARING FOR PEOPLE

What happens if someone at an Antarctic research station gets sick or hurt? Fortunately, there's a clinic with medicine, supplies, and equipment to treat many illnesses and **injuries**. There's even a place to perform operations. At some stations, the doctor can **videoconference** with distant doctors for advice.

The clinic doctor faces extreme challenges. A serious illness or injury could occur suddenly. The right medicine, supplies, or equipment for a particular illness or injury might not be on hand. The doctor must work with what they have. It's a job that requires years of experience dealing with unexpected, often serious problems in challenging conditions.

THE WORST CASE

In 1999, the doctor at one of the US Antarctic stations discovered she had cancer, a serious, often deadly condition. It was winter, so the weather was too bad for a plane to rescue her. Even though flying was dangerous, a plane dropped medicine to her. She treated herself while continuing her duties as station doctor.

This dentist from McMurdo Station traveled to the Amundsen-Scott South Pole Station to meet a patient.

To keep well, people also need to eat well. That's especially true in extreme conditions such as those found in Antarctica. So the preparation of food at research stations is an important job. Larger stations usually have a chef. At smaller stations, people often take turns doing the cooking.

The chef usually must work with dried, canned, or frozen food. In fact, because food may be stored outside, even the dried and canned food may become frozen! Fresh fruits, vegetables, and meat are only available occasionally. Yet the chefs always work hard to prepare healthy, appealing meals. They may even bake cakes to celebrate birthdays!

igloo made to protect food from sunlight

This Antarctic greenhouse produces green vegetables for the South Pole's winter workers.

FOOD IN THE FIELD

Scientists going into the field for 1 day may make a sandwich to take along. For several days in the field, the chef may prepare meals for them to take along and reheat later. For longer periods in the field, they'll likely have dried foods that they'll prepare using melted snow for water.

AN EXTREME WORK TIMETABLE

You probably view summer as the time to relax and have fun. However, it's when most research and construction are done at Antarctic research stations. That's because winter weather is too bad for work, and it's too dark, since the sun disappears completely! So people are very busy during summer. They know they have only a limited time to get their work done.

Work may start around 8:00 in the morning and go until 8:00 in the evening. Sometimes, people work even longer. For example, unloading a supply ship may mean working until late at night for several days. The clock is always ticking.

MAKING UP FOR LYING UP

Work hours for scientists in the field can get very long. Time spent "lying up" in their tents because of bad weather is time lost for their research. So when the weather finally clears, they work around the clock to make up for the lost time.

Scientists collect samples in the Transantarctic Mountains. This team found rocks that may prove that East Antarctica was once connected to the western United States.

TIME FOR FUN

Even with the hard work and long days, people find time to relax and have fun. They read, watch DVDs, play board games, and exercise on gym equipment. They ski, climb mountains, ride snowmobiles, play sports, and even take walks. Some even climb down into crevasses!

Those who spend the winter brighten the long darkness with special ceremonies. They celebrate sundown on the last day the sun rises. They celebrate midwinter with a week of special events, ending with a feast.

Now that you've learned something about life at an Antarctic research station, do you think you'd like to go?

New Year's Day celebration at McMurdo Station

THE TOP OF THE WORLD

The Arctic region around the North Pole differs from Antarctica. There's no land—just sea ice. But Canada, Russia, and other countries have land close to the Arctic ice, and polar research stations are found there, too. These stations work much like those in Antarctica, and scientists there study many of the same things.

29

GLOSSARY

climate change: long-term change in Earth's climate, caused partly by human activities such as burning oil and natural gas

ecosystem: all the living things in an area

equipment: machines, instruments, and tools needed for an activity or operation

generator: a machine that uses moving parts to produce electrical energy

geology: the science that studies the history of Earth and its life as recorded in rocks

injury: hurt or harm

mechanic: a person who builds and fixes cars and other vehicles

meteorologist: someone who studies weather, climate, and the atmosphere

research: studying to find something new

technical: having special knowledge of machines or instruments

vehicle: an object that carries people or goods, such as a car or plane

videoconference: the holding of a meeting among people at different locations by means of audio and video signals

FOR MORE INFORMATION

Books

Friedman, Mel. *Antarctica.* New York, NY: Children's Press, 2009.

Latta, Sara L. *Ice Scientist: Careers in the Frozen Antarctic.* Berkeley Heights, NJ: Enslow Publishers, 2009.

Walker, Sally M. *Frozen Secrets: Antarctica Revealed.* Minneapolis, MN: Carolrhoda Books, 2010.

Websites

Arctic and Antarctic: An Overview of NSF Research
www.nsf.gov/news/overviews/arcticantarctic/index.jsp
Learn about research funded by the National Science Foundation in both Antarctica and the Arctic.

ICE: Climate Expeditions
climate-expeditions.org
Read stories and see videos about climate research in Antarctica.

POLENET: The Polar Earth Observing Network
www.polenet.org
Watch video podcasts about life at a remote Antarctic field camp.

INDEX